Franklin Makes a Deal

From an episode of the animated TV series *Franklin* produced by Nelvana Limited, Neurones France s.a.r.l. and Neurones Luxembourg S.A.

Based on the *Franklin* books by Paulette Bourgeois and Brenda Clark.

TV tie-in adaptation written by Sharon Jennings and illustrated by Sean Jeffrey, Alice Sinkner, Jelena Sisic, and Shelley Southern.

Based on the TV episode *Franklin's Bargain*, written by Brian Lasenby.

ISBN 0-439-43126-3

Text copyright © 2003 by Contextx Inc.
Illustrations copyright © 2003 Brenda Clark Illustrator Inc.

12 11 10 9 8 7 6 5 4 3 2 1   3 4 5 6 7/0

Printed in the U.S.A.   23
First Scholastic printing, December 2003

Kids Can Press is a *Corus*™ Entertainment company

Franklin Makes a Deal

SCHOLASTIC INC.

New York Toronto London Auckland Sydney
Mexico City New Delhi Hong Kong Buenos Aires

FRANKLIN had lots of things to play with.
He had puzzles and games, blocks and balls. He
had a bicycle and a toboggan and skates. But he
didn't have a Super-Duper Spy Kit. Franklin really
wanted a Super-Duper Spy Kit, and so he made a
super-duper deal.

Franklin rushed up the lane and into his backyard.

"Dad, Dad!" he panted. "The new Super-Duper Spy Kit is in the toy shop. I just have to get one."

"How much does it cost?" his father asked.

"That's the problem," replied Franklin. "It costs ten dollars, and I've only got five."

"That is a problem," agreed his father.

But Franklin had an idea.

"I'll do an extra chore," he said. "You can pay me five dollars."

"Five dollars is a lot of money," his father replied. "It would have to be a pretty big chore."

"That's okay," said Franklin. "I'd do anything for a Super-Duper Spy Kit."

His father thought for a minute.

"The fence needs painting," he finally said.

Franklin looked at the fence. It stretched all the way around the yard.

"Have we got a deal?" his father asked.

Franklin gulped . . . and nodded.

Franklin ran into the house and emptied his piggy bank.

"What's going on?" asked his mother.

Franklin explained the deal he had made with his father.

"So now I'm going to the store to buy a Super-Duper Spy Kit," he finished.

Franklin found his father in the backyard.

"Can I have my five dollars?" he asked.

"First you paint the fence, then I pay you the money," replied his father.

"But . . ." began Franklin.

"No buts," his father said. "That's the deal."

He handed Franklin a can of paint and a brush.

Franklin lugged the
paint over to the fence
and got started.

In a little while, his wrist was
stiff and his back hurt, his neck
ached and his knees were sore.

An hour later, he was hot
and tired and bored. But then
he thought about the Super-Duper
Spy Kit.

"It's worth all this work,"
Franklin decided.

By midafternoon, Franklin wasn't so sure. He was only halfway around the yard.

He felt even worse when Beaver and Fox came by to visit. They both had their Super-Duper Spy Kits.

"When are you getting one?" Fox asked.

"As soon as I finish painting," replied Franklin.

Beaver looked at the fence.

"That's going to take forever," she said.

But then Franklin had an idea.

"I'd be finished in no time if you both helped me," he said.

Fox and Beaver looked at each other.

"Please," begged Franklin. "It's lots of fun."

"Fun?" said Beaver. "It looks like work."

"Well, it's a little bit of work," Franklin agreed. "But you'll like painting."

Fox and Beaver looked at each other again.

"I'll get you some cookies," offered Franklin.

"It's a deal!" said Fox and Beaver.

Franklin found two more paintbrushes. Then he ran into the house.

"Beaver and Fox are helping me paint," he told his mother. "I promised them cookies."

"These cookies are for the school bake sale," his mother replied.

"Please?" begged Franklin.

His mother thought for a moment.

"Here's the deal," she said. "You can have some of these cookies if you clean up the dishes. Then I can make another batch for the bake sale."

Franklin looked at the sink full of bowls and spoons, measuring cups and cookie sheets. Then he looked out the window at the fence.

"Okay," he mumbled.

Franklin was filling the sink when Bear came to the door. Franklin explained what was going on.

"I have to wash the dishes so my mom will give me cookies so I can give some to Beaver and Fox so they'll help me paint the fence so my dad will give me five dollars so I can buy a Super-Duper Spy Kit."

"Wow!" said Bear.

Then Franklin had another idea.

"If you wash the dishes, I could keep painting. Then I could get to the store today to buy a Super-Duper Spy Kit," he said.

Bear thought for a moment.

"I'll do the dishes if you let me play with your Super-Duper Spy Kit," he said.

"It's a deal!" said Franklin.

Franklin went back to painting with Beaver and Fox. Soon Bear joined them.

"All done," Bear said.

Franklin ran inside.

"The dishes are done," he called to his mother.

Franklin grabbed handfuls of cookies and hurried back to his friends.

"Have a cookie, Bear," he said. "And here's your paintbrush."

"Hey!" said Bear. "Painting wasn't part of the deal."

"It is now!" laughed Beaver.

In no time at all, the fence was painted. Franklin's father gave him five dollars.

"Let's go!" cried Franklin. "Now I have ten dollars!"

The friends ran all the way to the toy shop.

There was a big sign in the window.
The sign read

SUPER-DUPER DEAL!

SUPER-DUPER SPY KITS ARE
ON SALE!

REGULAR PRICE $10.00

NOW ONLY $5.00

Franklin bought two.

"Gee, Franklin," said Bear. "Thanks for buying
me my very own Super-Duper Spy Kit."
Franklin laughed.
"How could I turn down a deal like that?"
he said.